Jack and the Magnificent Ugly Stick

Joshua Goudie
art by Craig Goudie

Tuckamore Books
a Creative Publishers imprint

St. John's, Newfoundland and Labrador
2016

Canada Council   Conseil des Arts
for the Arts   du Canada

Canada

Newfoundland
Labrador

We gratefully acknowledge the financial support of the Canada Council for
the Arts, the Government of Canada through the Canada Book Fund (CBF),
and the Government of Newfoundland and Labrador through the Department of
Business, Tourism, Culture and Rural Development for our publishing program.

Cover Design and Illustrations by Craig Goudie
Printed on acid-free paper

Published by
TUCKAMORE BOOKS
an imprint of CREATIVE BOOK PUBLISHING
a Transcontinental Inc. associated company
P.O. Box 8660, Stn. A
St. John's, Newfoundland and Labrador A1B 3T7

Printed in Canada by:
Transcontinental Inc.

Library and Archives Canada Cataloguing in Publication

Goudie, Joshua, 1985-, author
    Jack and the magnificent ugly stick / Joshua Goudie ; art
by Craig Goudie.

ISBN 978-1-77103-090-8 (hardback)

    I. Goudie, Craig, 1960-, illustrator II. Title.

PS8613.O824J33 2016   jC813'.6   C2016-904000-3

For Ron Hynes; the man of a thousand songs!

With his rod in one hand, his tackle box in the other and his rubber boots on his feet, Jack had everything he needed for a fishing trip.

Unfortunately, Jack's grandmother was not having the same luck. "Oh dear!" said Jack's grandmother as she rummaged through box after box in the backyard shed. "I don't think we'll be able to go fishing after all."

"Why not?" asked Jack.

"Because," his grandmother said. "I can only find one of my rubber boots. I'll go check in the house but, until I can find my other boot, this fishing trip will have to wait." As she took the path back to the house she added, "I was so looking forward to this too. Oh dear."

Jack knew how much his grandmother loved fishing and was sad that she wouldn't be able to go. So, with that in mind, Jack decided that he would look high and he would look low until he found his grandmother's missing boot.

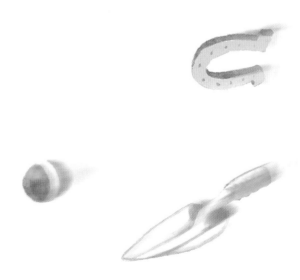

Jack took off down the road and headed for the beach. "Maybe she left it there after our last fishing trip," he said to himself. But no matter how hard he looked, Jack could not find his grandmother's missing boot. "It must be somewhere else," he said.

That's when Jack heard a voice. "Lost something?"

Jack turned around and saw his friend Matthew standing on the beach rocks.

"I'm trying to find my grandmother's missing boot," said Jack.

"Hmm," said Matthew. "Well I've been on the beach all day and I haven't seen any missing boots. But good luck finding it. There's not much you can do with one boot except make an ugly stick."

"An ugly stick?" asked Jack. "What's an ugly stick?"

"It's a musical instrument," said Matthew. "It's something you play to make other people dance."

This got Jack thinking. With only one rubber boot, Jack knew his grandmother wouldn't be able to go fishing. But Jack also knew that if there was one thing his grandmother liked more than fishing, it was dancing. So, with that in mind, Jack hatched a new plan.

"How do you make an ugly stick?" asked Jack.

"Well," said Matthew, "the first thing you need is a long piece of driftwood. If you can find me one, I'll show you."

When Jack came back, he was carrying a piece of driftwood almost as tall as himself. "Perfect," said Matthew. "Let's make you an ugly stick!" Then in a flash, Matthew flipped the boot upside down, popped it on the piece of driftwood and hammered the two together. "There," he said, handing the stick over to Jack. "Your very own ugly stick!"

Jack held the stick. It looked strange. "How do I make music with this?" he asked.

"Just hold on tight and bang the boot on the ground," said Matthew.

THUMP! THUMP! THUMP!

"That sounds great!" said Matthew. "Don't stop now!"

So Jack kept going.

THUMP! THUMP-A! THUMP! THUMP-A!

THUMP! THUMP! THUMP!

"You're a natural," said Matthew.

"Thanks," said Jack.

"Hey! I know," Matthew said. "Why don't we play a song together?"

"A song?" asked Jack.

"Sure," said Matthew. "I've got my fiddle here. We can be just like a real band!"

With that, Matthew brought out his fiddle. Then he held it close to his chin and began to play. The music was so much fun that Jack decided to play along.

THUMP! THUMP-A! THUMP! THUMP-A!
THUMP! THUMP! THUMP!

"Wow!" said Matthew when their song was over. "We've got the start of a great band here."

"You really think so?" asked Jack.

"I know so," said Matthew.

"Then would you mind coming with me to my grandmother's house?" asked Jack. "She's sad because she can't go fishing today but maybe we can cheer her up with a song!"

"Sounds good to me," said Matthew.

"Well come on," said Jack, and the pair took off for Jack's grandmother's house.

At Geraldine's chicken farm, Jack and Matthew had to stop and catch their breath.

"That's a fine looking ugly stick," said Geraldine who was taking a break from feeding her chickens. "But, if I can make a suggestion, I think that ugly stick could use a tin can."

"A tin can?" asked Jack.

"Sure," said Geraldine. "Let me show you."

"There," said Geraldine, handing the stick over to Jack. "Give it a try."

Jack held the stick. Now it looked even stranger. "How do I make music with this?"

"Just hold tight, bang the boot on the ground and flick the can with your finger," said Geraldine.

THUMP! THUMP! TING!

"That's it!" said Geraldine. "Don't stop now!"

So Jack kept going.

THUMP! THUMP! TING! THUMP! THUMP! TING!

THUMP! THUMP-A! THUMP! THUMP-A!

THUMP! THUMP! TING!

"Amazing," said Geraldine. "You're a natural."

"Thanks," said Jack.

"Say," said Geraldine, "why don't we play a song together? I can grab my accordion and we'll be just like a real band!"

Geraldine ran into the farmhouse and came back out with her accordion. Then she rested it on her knee and began to play.

The music was so much fun that Matthew joined in on his fiddle and Jack played along using his ugly stick.

THUMP! THUMP! TING! THUMP! THUMP! TING!

THUMP! THUMP-A! THUMP! THUMP-A!

THUMP! THUMP! TING!

"Wow!" said Geraldine when their song was over. "We've got the start of a great band here."

"You really think so?" asked Jack.

"I know so," said Geraldine.

"Then would you mind joining us?" asked Jack. "We're going to cheer up my grandmother with a song since she can't go fishing today."

"You bet I will," said Geraldine.

"Well, come on," said Jack, and they all took off for Jack's grandmother's house.

When they reached Andrew's store, Jack, Matthew and Geraldine needed to stop for some water.

"That's a magnificent ugly stick," said Andrew as he gave them all drinks. "But, if I can make a suggestion, I think that ugly stick could use a few bottle caps."

"Bottle caps?" asked Jack.

"Sure!" said Andrew. "Let me just grab some from inside."

"There," said Andrew, handing the stick over to Jack. "Give it a try."

Jack held the stick. Now it looked even stranger. "How do I make music with this?"

"Just hold tight, bang the boot on the ground, flick the can with your finger and give the bottle caps a shake," said Andrew.

THUMP! TING! CLINK!

"There you go!" said Andrew. "Don't stop now!"

So Jack kept going.

THUMP! TING! CLINK! THUMP! TING! CLINK!

THUMP! THUMP-A! THUMP! THUMP-A!

THUMP! TING! CLINK!

"Fantastic," said Andrew. "You're a natural."

"Thanks," said Jack.

"Say," said Andrew, "why don't I grab my guitar and we can all play a song? Then we'll be just like a real band!"

With that, Andrew ran into his store and came back out with his guitar. Then he tossed the strap over his shoulder and began to play.

The music was so much fun that Matthew joined in on his fiddle, Geraldine squeezed her accordion and Jack played along using his ugly stick.

THUMP! TING! CLINK! THUMP! TING! CLINK!

THUMP! THUMP-A! THUMP! THUMP-A!

THUMP! TING! CLINK!

"Wow!" said Andrew when their song was over. "We've got the start of a great band here."

"You really think so?" asked Jack.

"I know so," said Andrew.

"Well, we're going to play a song for my grandmother," said Jack. "We're trying to cheer her up since she can't go fishing today. Would you like to come along?"

"You've got it," said Andrew.

"Then come on," said Jack, and they all took off towards Jack's grandmother's house.

"Jack!" said Jack's grandmother when they all burst through the door. "Where have you been? I was worried sick."

"Sorry," said Jack. "I went to look for your boot but, when I couldn't find it, I made an ugly stick instead! After all, there's not much you can do with one boot except make an ugly stick. And now we're going to cheer you up with a song!"

"But Jack," said Jack's grandmother, "I found my other boot under my bed. It was there the whole time."

"Oh Jack! How did you know?" said Jack's grandmother. "I always liked dancing more than fishing anyway!"

Artist's photo credits (l-r): Keenan Goddard-Donovan, Chris Ledrew and Graham Kennedy

Just as each musical instrument has a special sound, it also has a unique look. Maybe no instrument proves this better than the ugly stick.

In many parts of Newfoundland and Labrador, ugly sticks are a common sight at concerts, kitchen parties and just about anywhere music is made. While fiddles, accordions and guitars play the melody of a song, the rhythm is kept by a person playing the ugly stick.

Part of the fun of an ugly stick is that no two are alike. In fact, most people make them out of things they find around their home. Whether you want to make a noise or decorate, you can add just about anything to an ugly stick. Hey! Why not ask a parent or a teacher to help you make your very own?

These days, musicians in Newfoundland and Labrador play music with their very own unique look and sound. Artists like Matthew Hornell, "The Once" (Geraldine Hollett, Andrew Dale and Phil Churchill) and "Fortunate Ones" (Andrew James O'Brien and Catherine Allan) have found great success playing shows all around the world. If you haven't heard them, give them a listen. Then, maybe start your very own band, dream big and see where the music takes you!

Michael Venn photo

Joshua Goudie was born in Grand Falls-Windsor and now lives and writes in St. John's. His work has been published in *The Telegram* as well as in several Cuffer anthologies. In 2013, he was short-listed for the Newfoundland and Labrador Credit Union's Fresh Fish Award.
Joshua enjoys playing mandolin and drums.

...Josh is Craig's son.

Craig Goudie has been working as a visual artist for over thirty years, producing work for galleries, serving on local and provincial arts-related boards and teaching high school art. His artwork hangs in government, corporate and private collections.
Craig enjoys singing and playing piano.

Joanne Goudie photo

...Craig is Josh's dad.